ISBN 978-1-80352-211-1

Cover design by: Aleah Lane Swift and Denice Allen
Library of Congress Control Number: 2018675309
Printed in the United Kingdom

Dedication

I thank God for all the inspiration, opportunities and ideas that led to the creation of this book.

I dedicate this book to my mum for all the support that she has given me turning my ideas into a reality and my dad for supporting my Animal Fusions business.

Contents

Foreword from Israel

My name is Israel. I'm ten years old and I'm an author. The Animal Fusions world was inspired by an animal fact book that I was gifted. After reading it I started creating animal fusions. I put two different animals together to make a drawing of a new character.

I did many drawings like this. I would draw every day because it was fun for me. My first batch of drawings was done when I was supposed to be in bed. I had a special pen that had a light that came on when you were using it. My parents thought I was asleep but I was drawing!

I like reading and I like making up stories in my head. Now I want to share my stories with other people. I want them to enjoy my stories and laugh.

Chapter 1

As he brought the spoon to his mouth, it shook because of the freezing cold. Though it was evening, he crunched on his favourite cereal. There wasn't much choice of what to eat in this hideaway, but he felt full and grateful that his mum and dad had gotten him enough food, but he was cold. As Bobfox finished slurping the last of his milk, he thought of his parents.

"If daddy and I don't come after a while, your big brother, Reinafox, will come and get you," Mum assured him. He had felt sad when she said that because if they didn't come back from the war, that meant they had died. At the same time, he felt safe because he knew that he would be looked after either way. Reinafox was strong, bold and courageous. When Reinafox was around, he was always safe. Reinafox had his powers. Everyone had their powers apart from Bobfox...

Bobfox thought of bedtimes at home. He got to speak to his Mum and not feel lonely. It was hard for him not to have hot showers. He'd never lived in the wild before. He saw wild bobfoxes and reinafoxes licking themselves on the TV. After five weeks, he smelled himself. He smelled bad, of rotten chicken and sweaty pants! Bobfox's nose twitched, and his little face scrunched up with disgust as he sniffed again.

"Eeewwwww! I stink!" He really needed a shower.

"Mummy, Daddy! Please come back," Bobfox pleaded to the air. The wind howled but didn't bring back an answer. His shoulders slumped and his head hung in sorrow as he sighed. Bobfox didn't want to think that the worst had happened...

He wiped his face with the raggedy fur on his arm and carried his empty bowl across the room, putting it on the wooden bench. He wiped it dry with the same cloth he had been using for days. It was starting to become skanky. He didn't really want to use it. The cloth used to be white, but after weeks of using it to wipe out the same bowl after each meal, it had become a dingy, grimy grey. There were crumbs and bits of his favourite cereal that had dried on the fluffy material, so that he now wasn't sure if he was really cleaning anything anymore. It really needed to be washed.

Bobfox gave an anxious look at his diminishing water supply. He didn't know when or if anyone was coming for him. He needed to make sure that he had water to drink for as long as possible.

"But how long will I be alone here?" he wondered out loud. As usual, he got no answer.

A tired and depressed Bobfox placed his one bowl and spoon next to his only knife and fork set on the wooden bench, while his mind continued spinning with never-ending, unanswered questions. His disordered imagination was throwing rapid images of his parents, Reinafox, the battlefield and everything that could have happened. His mind and body were exhausted.

Bobfox trudged across the floor to his bed and climbed in. He pulled the covers over his head in the hope that he could sleep... quickly.

Chapter 2

Four pairs of dark, hollow eye sockets seemed to be staring at him. The skulls' creepy smiles freaked him out as they just lay there on the fire-scorched ground. The day was turning into evening and grey clouds rolled over the sky, covering Bobfox with a blanket of hopelessness and despair. He hadn't seen anyone he knew yet, but he could just feel that something bad was about to happen.

His eyes probed the battlefield and saw the many corpses all over – dead heroes and villains who had fought to win but failed to stay alive to see the end result.

Boom! Thunder exploded in the sky. It sounded very close. The noise terrified Bobfox. He immediately looked for the nearest place to hide from the monster in the sky. He dived behind a large, jagged and hideous rock. His fur pricked up and his heart felt like it could jump out of his chest.

Before he had a chance to catch his breath, the sound of a thousand arrows whizzing through the air, ready to slice through their enemies, made him hold it. Eventually, he let it all out and found a little bit of courage to peek over the top of his rock cover to see what was happening.

Still shaking with fear, Bobfox stared in the direction the arrows had come from. He was terror-stricken with what he saw...

A black, horrifying and shapeless blob of evil seemed to be moving quickly towards a target. As it got closer, it

seemed to be a lot of little dark blobs all bunched together. Bobfox couldn't pick out individual figures in their darkness but he could see terrifying eyes. Thousands of big, blood red eyes stared maliciously at their target and they carried on heading in the same direction.

Crash! Suddenly, a bolt of lightning lit up the darkened sky for a second. In that second, Bobfox wished he hadn't been looking. He saw pure nastiness. Sharp knife-like teeth shone like diamonds in the deep caves of their faces. They looked like they wanted to destroy everything around them. Bobfox thought that they could.

He scanned in the other direction and what he saw filled him with hope. Reinafox! Wolferine! Coyolf! His heroes were there courageously facing the wall of evil. They had their shields in front of them. The arrows of evil broke into pieces when they hit them. Bobfox felt bolder. Evil wasn't going to win! Not against his big brother and his hero army of friends!

As he watched the army of heroes holding their ground, he gasped. He couldn't believe what he was seeing. Could it really be them?

"Mum!" he shouted. "Dad!" he shrieked.

They didn't seem to hear him. It was definitely them. He wanted to hug them so much it made him want to run across the battlefield. He didn't even think about the fact that he didn't have any armour on to protect himself.

'Mum! Dad!" He screamed his lungs out and started running towards them beaming. They heard him then, but their faces were not beaming. They looked petrified.

"Bobfox! No!" his Mum cried out in panic. "What are you doing here?" Dad exclaimed fearfully.

Bobfox was not listening. He was so happy to see them again. He kept running towards his parents, his safety.

The evil mob were preparing to fire their next round of fiery arrows, but Bobfox couldn't see them. The heroes got their shields ready.

Bobfox kept on running. His parents lowered their shields and dashed towards their beloved son to try and save him. Then everything slowed down.

He heard the deadly arrows being fired and he froze with fear. His Mum and Dad hadn't reached him yet, so they hurled their shields in his direction. They landed around him like a protective shelter.

He heard the crashes and bangs of the arrows breaking into pieces as they hit the shields. There was a small gap between the two shields protecting him that allowed him to see what he wished he could unsee. Hundreds of arrows hit his exposed parents and pinned them to the ground.

"Noooooooooo!" Bobfox let out a cry of anguish so loud and horrible that everything disappeared into black.

"Mum! Daaaaaaad!"

That last cry woke him up with a fright.

The scruffy fur on his face was wet with tears. He was back in his bed in the cold and lonely hideout. He curled up into a ball and wiped away the tears with his paws, but when they kept coming, he allowed them to flow freely. He was tired – tired of waiting for someone to come; tired of being alone; tired of not knowing if his family was dead or alive.

He would go back to sleep now, but in the morning, he was busting out of here.

Chapter 3

Bobfox trudged along, exhausted from walking through the countryside for the last seven days. He wasn't totally sure where he was going. He was following a country road he had found. Roads meant traffic. Traffic meant more fusion beings. More fusion beings could lead him to information about where his family was.

His cereal had run out a day ago and now his stomach was rumbling loudly. He had no money, and he hadn't seen anything he could eat for ages. He had managed to get some water in his bottle from a stream he had passed. That stream had been like heaven on Earth. He had dived straight in!

"Woohooo! No more stinky Bobfox!!" he had shouted delightfully, as he splashed around with joy. It had been his first wash in ages and had felt amazing. He shook his shiny grey fur to get rid of the extra water and then stretched out in the sunshine to dry off completely. That had been a good day. He sighed happily.

That was also the last day he had eaten properly. Bobfox sighed again, but this time he felt glum. He needed to find food soon and he needed a way to speed up his journey. Just then, he heard the hum of a wagon. His ears pricked up in the direction of the sound. It was nearby and it was stopping.

"Maybe it's someone who can help me," Bobfox thought. He ran towards the sound.

He came to the roadside and saw a small, blue wagon truck. There were two seats in front and the back was like an open cart. Whatever was in there was covered with a beige sackcloth. Bobfox looked on from the safety of a bush across the road.

The driver got out of the wagon truck and stretched his body towards the sky. He was old and a big guy. He looked scary and mean. His body was large and his raggedy orange- brown hair was like wildfire. His arms seemed too long for his body. Bobfox had never seen such a fusion being. His large belly was held in by old farmer dungarees, which he was undoing.

He was looking around as though to check if anyone was looking. He looked angry.

"Has he seen me?" Bobfox quivered. But then the scraggy farmer backed into a bush, pulled down his dungarees and crouched.

"Yuck!" Bobfox said, all grossed out. "He's doing a poo!"

Then he had an idea. That wagon would really help to speed up his journey, but the big guy looked too mean for him to ask for a ride. "He'd probably say no," Bobfox reasoned. "I need to get on that wagon," he said quietly to himself.He looked at the wagon with determination, and stole a glance at the cranky farmer who was squeezing his eyes shut as he forced out the brown bricks.

"Now's my chance!" His shiny black nose twitched, his eyes zoned in on his target and he pounded one paw into the other. He took one more glance at the crouched farmer, bolted silently towards the back of the wagon and ducked behind the wheel. His grey and black tipped ears swivelled left and right listening out for sudden movements. Hearing nothing new, he jumped up, landing lightly on the back of the wagon. Keeping as low as possible, he snuck under the beige sackcloth. His heart was pounding.

"I did it!" Bobfox exclaimed in his thoughts. He was pleased with himself. He heard the farmer return to the

13

wagon. The door banged shut, the engine turned on and they were off.

Suddenly, his nose was hit with so many delicious smells it was like a party in his nostrils. Carrots, watermelons, apples, plums and bananas! It was a bit dark under this blanket, but his nose wasn't lying. His rumbling stomach now roared. He was drooling. He knew the food didn't belong to him, but surely the cranky farmer wouldn't mind. He was sooooo hungry! He would eat a lot...

Minutes later, Bobfox had eaten a little of everything on the back of that wagon. The energy rush made him excited, and he soon forgot that he was meant to be hiding...

Suddenly, the wagon's tires screeched to a halt. Before Bobfox could take a breath, the beige sackcloth was ripped off leaving him all exposed. He froze.

"Oi! What are you doing in my wagon kid?" the angry fusion being demanded loudly.

As Bobfox shook with ice cold terror, the farmer's eyes searched the back of his wagon. His eyes seemed to turn red.

"Why, you little brat!" His extra-long furry arm reached out to grab the little food thief, but Bobfox was too quick. He ran for his life and kept running into the nearby woods. He stopped only when he couldn't see the dusty road anymore and the scary giant was far away.

Bobfox leaned against a tree trunk, bent over and tried to catch his breath. He was panting hard. All he wanted to do was find his family.

"Why couldn't he have been nice to me?" he thought. "Couldn't he see that I'm just a kid?" Bobfox began to get angry. "Why couldn't he just try and help? Isn't that what adults are supposed to do?"

His thoughts were spinning round. "If this is what adults are like now," he said to himself out loud, "then I will take care of myself. I'll do whatever it takes to survive." Bobfox slumped against the tree and rested a while.

Chapter 4

Bobfox stopped again to catch his breath. The day was warm with little breeze and his fur was sticky with sweat. He had to keep going further away from the country roads to visit the stream to drink and cool down, but he didn't want to keep going off track because it was making his journey longer. So, he kept on as long as possible before taking a break. It was getting harder though. It had been three days since he had escaped from the angry farmer and three days since he had eaten the scrumptious, delicious food.

Bobfox's mouth started watering as he remembered the smells. He hadn't seen any fruit on the trees the past few days. The water from the stream satisfied his thirst, but he couldn't go on much longer without food. His stomach growled so loud he felt pain.

He leaned his back against a tree, sighing deeply and let his head fall back onto the tree to rest. As he looked up, he saw something at the top of the tree in front of him. He put his paw above his eyes to shield them from the sun and squinted to make sure he was seeing clearly. Right at the top of the tree were three luscious, golden apples.

His eyes opened wide. He rubbed them to make sure it was an illusion. It wasn't. The apples were still there. He crouched down low and got ready to jump as high as he could to start climbing the tree. The lowest branch was quite high up and he would need all his energy to reach it. Bobfox jumped up with all that he had inside of him and...

...His little paws scraped and scratched at the trunk, but he fell back down to the ground, annoyed. He focused on the apples again, crouched determined to get the food and...

…His paws scratched and scraped as before and he even gave a little growl, but still he failed.

"Damn it!" Bobfox hissed. He was hungry but he didn't have the energy to reach the snack right in front of him. He needed to eat!

"You're not going to beat me, tree!" He pounded one paw into the other. His breathing was a little faster now and he was feeling weak, but he was going to get those apples! But once again, he failed. And again and again and again.

Bobfox gasped for breath wildly as he was bent over. He didn't have the energy to reach the top. This was not fair! He had been abandoned in the hideout; he was alone with no one to help him; no one was there that cared for him;

17

the angry farmer tried to hurt him and now these simple apples were teasing him.

His paws clenched into fists; like a volcano, he shook and a savage scream erupted from his mouth. With all his frustration, he sliced and diced at the tree trunk with his paws. Then something strange happened...

His arms and paws seemed to go at supersonic speed while the rest of his body stayed normal. In a few seconds, he must have sliced at that tree trunk a thousand times, and by the time it stopped... CRASH! The tree broke at the trunk and fell down flat.

Bobfox's eyes were now huge and his mouth hung wide open. He looked from the fallen tree to his paws and back again.

"What in the world ...?" he exclaimed! He remembered his hunger and went to get the apples that were now on the ground. As he ate them, he remembered again what had just happened.

"Could this be my power?" he wondered. His Mum, Dad and Reinafox had always told him that he would get his powers one day. They warned him that he should use them for good and not evil. Thinking of them made him a little sad again.

"How could this power be used for good?" he thought. His mind was whizzing fast.

For now, he was happy with the snack in his stomach. He could carry on a little longer. He had a mission to accomplish. He would find out what happened to his family.

Chapter 5

The wind whooshed through Bobfox's whiskers as he sped down a small hill section of the quiet country road. This penny board was making his journey faster and less painful. It was a fun way to travel. As he was on the hill, he could have all four paws rested on the board while gravity did all the work. He wasn't proud of the way he had gotten it, but it was definitely helping him out.

Bobfox stopped by a patch of open grass. He needed a snack. The grass was as soft as a cushion as he sat on it. He took his new black backpack off his shoulders and unzipped it. He reached inside and selected one of the packs of breakfast bars. He chose the frosty flakes flavour, unwrapped it and took a big bite. Bobfox savoured the taste and the increase in energy. When he closed his eyes, the morning sun shone down on him. His mind went to the days before...

...

It was already dark when he had found the mini supermarket. He was sick with hunger. It had been a whole day since he had discovered his powers. Those apples could only feed him for so long and he was very tired from travelling. The bright blue billboard had invited him:

We have food. We have toys.
We have everything you need for a long journey.

This was exactly what Bobfox needed! But the store was closed and he didn't have any money anyway. The place was deserted with no one around for miles. The shop was closed down with metal shutters locked over the doors and windows. A bad thought that made him feel guilty came to his mind, but the more he thought about it, the more he saw that it could help him.

"If it helps me find my parents, it can't be that bad of an idea I guess," Bobfox reasoned to himself. Then it seemed like a conversation broke out in his head between his good side and a darker side.

"It's not a bad thing to steal if it helps you survive..."

"You could wait until morning and speak to the shopkeeper. They could help you. You don't have to steal."

"Remember what happened with the farmer? Adults don't want to help you! You're alone."

"Remember Mum, Dad and Reinafox," the softer voice said. "What did they tell you about when you got your powers?" Bobfox frowned as he remembered out loud what they had said every time he asked about when he would get his powers.

"You have to always do what's right. We all have powers, but we must use them to do good, to serve others."

"It's not like you're going to do this all the time is it?" The thought battle continued. "You just need a few supplies to help you get where you're going. Who is here to serve you? You have to serve yourself!"

Bobfox agreed more and more with this voice. Who would know it was him? He would try not to do too much damage, but his new powers would help him get in and out quickly. He had made up his mind as he stealthily went up to the main shutter and got ready to slice and dice his way in.

Bobfox had practised controlling his destructive powers over the last day, so he was feeling very confident about doing this with as little damage as possible. He stood in front of the lock and calmed himself, focused on that lock alone and... SCREECH! CLANG! He sliced and diced, and the lock shattered into a thousand pieces. He was in.

23

He would only take what he needed...

Bobfox left the shop tidy, closed the door and pulled in the shutter. His new rucksack was full of food and other supplies to keep him alive for his journey. It was a surprise to find the penny board for sale. It was going to make his journey faster for sure. A part of him really wished that he hadn't had to do this, but the other part of him was feeling good as he had enough food for the first time since the hideout.

...

Bobfox shook his head and brought himself back to where he was. He finished the rest of his breakfast bar and got ready to move on again. He put on his backpack, picked up his penny board and headed back to the country road.

He hadn't been riding for longer than a few minutes when he spotted a young-looking fusion being sat down and leaning against a rock by the side of the road. He looked so exhausted and weak, it reminded Bobfox of how he had felt not so long ago. The fusion being looked bigger than Bobfox, but he wasn't threatened. He stopped rolling on his penny board and picked it up. He moved closer, but the fusion being did not make any sudden movements.

"Hi, my name is Bobfox. Are you okay?"

The fusion being slowly raised his head like it was too heavy for him. He opened his eyes and looked at Bobfox, trying figure out if he was in danger or not. Bobfox tried to look as friendly as possible.

"Are you hungry?" he said, as he began to take his bag off his shoulders. "I have some breakfast bars you can have."

Grateful and relieved, the black and muscular being sat up.

"Thank you." He wiped the sweat from his face. "I'm very hungry."

Bobfox handed him two breakfast bars and he guzzled them down so quickly that Bobfox felt sorry for him. He obviously had not eaten for ages. He handed him a bottle of water and that was gulped down almost in one. His orange-green eyes brightened as he smiled at Bobfox. He sighed happily and said, "Hi, I'm Wolfarilla."

"Pleased to meet you, I'm Bobfox." He sat on the grass next to him.

By the end of the hour, Bobfox and Wolfarilla were like best buddies. They were both looking for parents lost in the war. They were both alone and Wolfarilla had discovered the strangest power Bobfox had ever heard of. They travelled on together, feeling safer in their newfound friendship. The journey was still not going to be easy, but they had each other's company to make it better and that was enough for now.

Chapter 6

It was such an effort for them to travel down the narrow country road. The penny board allowed Bobfox to travel faster than when he was just walking, but he and his new best friend, Wolfarilla, were worn out and really hungry. They had been travelling together for two weeks now and Bobfox felt as though he had found another brother in Wolfarilla.

When he stood up tall, Wolfarilla could look a bit unnerving, but as soon as he smiled, he made everyone feel comfortable again. He was confident to approach others in a way that Bobfox wasn't. With his charm, Wolfarilla managed to get them a few rides with pleasant strangers who were travelling across the country. Bobfox had begun to realise that not all adults were like the cranky farmer. Some adults had even been able to answer a few of their questions.

Now they knew that there had been many deaths on both sides – the most that fusion beings had ever seen. The winning side fought for justice and freedom for all fusion beings. They wanted a world where all were clear on what was right and what was wrong. They wanted all beings to be responsible for their actions and to know that it was their duty to serve their community for the greater good. Those who led the victory were now known as the heroes.

It made them feel hopeful that the good side had won. But their parents hadn't come back for them... That old bad feeling started to return to Bobfox's stomach. This new information made the feeling that something bad had happened to his parents even more real. Bobfox sighed.

"Is there a list of the heroes that died in the war?" Wolfarilla questioned the kind stranger giving them a ride.

"There is a memorial wall in the Big City centre where they engraved the names of all the fallen heroes. They finished it about a month ago."

Bobfox and Wolfarilla rode with the stranger for a few hours before they went their separate ways. They needed to get to the Big City which was a few days car ride, but now they were out of supplies and in need of rest. They had spotted the signs for a nearby supermarket.

As it was night time, the store was closed and deserted. The shop had everything they needed, but they had no money and the shutters were down. An old thought battle went through Bobfox's mind, alongside the guilt of his final decision. As Bobfox used his well-practised powers to break through the shutters and enter the store, something moved in the shadows unseen by the two friends...

A pair of fierce, glowing green eyes scrutinised every move Bobfox and Wolfarilla made. Its sleek, golden, furry body moved carefully, undetected in the dark among the trees and bushes. Its large black wings were folded back and tightly tucked into its shoulder blades as it waited to make its move.

Meanwhile, Bobfox met Wolfarilla near the checkout. Their rucksacks were full. "Have you taken only what you need?" Bobfox asked.

"Yes, that's what we agreed right?"

"Good. Let's go then." Bobfox sighed heavily and they headed back towards the door. Wolfarilla tucked his new skateboard under his armpit as he followed Bobfox out of the store. He almost knocked him over when Bobfox suddenly stopped and froze in his tracks.

"Heeey!" Wolfarilla started, but then he saw what had made his friend stop so abruptly. They had been caught.

The fusion being blocking their exit stared at them with fierce, glowing green eyes and looked ready to pounce on them. But he said nothing.

Wolfarilla's heart beat so hard that it was almost painful and his breathing had quickly become shallow. They just couldn't get caught! Not now when they were close to finding out about their parents!! He thought it was weird when he first discovered his power, but he knew exactly what to do with it now.

He stretched out his muscly, black-haired arms and clenched his fists. He focused hard as he had practised before and the pin-like pointy spikes raised out of his skin. He pointed them in the direction of the threat and... whoosh! As he opened his hands, the spray of spikes flew through the air and headed towards their target. They only had a few seconds.

"Run! Now!" Wolfarilla pushed Bobfox into action and they started for the door. The creature didn't move. Then time seemed to slow down and what happened next was completely unexpected.

In the blink of an eye, two black gigantic wings unfolded from the fusion being's back. Then they flapped in front so quickly that you could barely see them move. But

Wolfarilla and Bobfox knew they were moving, as the strong wind they created sent them diving back into the supermarket. The spray of spikes had changed direction and were now attacking them! Bobfox's eyes were wide with surprise and fear. He peered at Wolfarilla from behind the till he had dived behind.

"Wow! What a power!" he gasped.

"It was kind of hard to explain." Wolfarilla poked his head above the till he was behind. "I've never used it against anyone before."

The footsteps of the scary black, winged stranger approaching made them both quiver and stop talking. What were they going to do now? How were they going to get out of this?

The stranger walked slowly and steadily into the supermarket entrance.

"I come in peace." He carried on moving, his eyes searching for the two youngsters. "I didn't mean to scare you. It was a reflex reaction to feeling attacked. I hope I didn't hurt you."

He walked cautiously towards the till area where he could see a pair of black pointy ears sticking up over a till a few rows ahead.

"I don't know where you are, but I promise I won't hurt you. I'm just a lonely old traveller looking for some food. I'm just so tired and hungry."

The fusion being gripped his belly looking very sad and sighed dramatically. A smaller pair of ears popped up over another till area and twitched nervously.

"My name is Dragalion. I have been travelling for weeks now. I'm heading towards the Big City to look for my son who fought in the war. I don't know if he survived the fighting..." Dragalion hung his head in exaggerated sorrow and waited.

Bobfox and Wolfarilla both raised their full heads and shoulders above their hiding places and looked at each other for assurance to show more of themselves. Bobfox gave Wolfarilla a nod and Wolfarilla nodded back.

They both slowly and hesitantly came out from their hiding places and stood next to each other, but still at a distance from Dragalion. They were not close enough to see him hiding a smirk.

"So, you're not here to punish us?" Bobfox asked.

Dragalion lifted his head quickly. "No, of course not!" he reassured them.

"I was so hungry and I was looking for a way to get some food. If you guys hadn't broken in here, I don't know when

33

I would have been able to eat again."

"We only took what we needed," Bobfox defended them. "If we had money, we would pay. Honest."

"But we don't have parents," Wolfarilla added. "We are on the way to the Big City as well. They fought in the war and we don't know what happened to them."

Dragalion put his paw over his heart. "Oh, you poor kids! You've only done what you had to," he said with sympathy. "I hope that you can see I'm only here to do the same. I would really appreciate it if you could show me around." He raised his right paw. "I promise to only take what I need as well. We're not bad thieves, are we?"

Bobfox and Wolfarilla looked each other in the eyes and gave another nod. They felt a little bad now for the way they had acted.

"We can help you," Wolfarilla said, as they headed towards the snacks aisle.

Dragalion followed them gratefully and as they filled his basket with supplies, he filled their ears with his story of how he had ended up on this journey for his son, the war hero.

34

The two young fusion beings were so interested by his story and understood the feeling of being alone and afraid. Dragalion was a lonely father looking for his son and they were sons looking for their parents. He understood them too. There was something about him that they trusted. As they left, he was no longer so scary to them. He seemed friendly and wanted to help protect them.

"This journey has just been crazy so far!" Bobfox's mind was spinning. "What an adventure! So many surprises. Who knows what will happen next?"

Chapter 7

"Weeeeeeee!" Little Bobfox squealed with excitement as he flew through the air with a basketball that seemed as big as the moon to his little paws. His flight to the big dunking hoop was held up by the reliable and strong arms of his big brother. These faithful arms had always made him feel safe, assured and supported. Reinafox was never far away.

His deep blue eyes looked up at his little brother sailing through the air in his arms with love. From the moment that Bobfox had been born into the family, Reinafox felt a big responsibility to protect him. He made a promise to the young cub that he would always be there for him no matter what.

The knock at the door shook Reinafox out of his memory. He blinked and cleared away the lump in his throat as he prepared to see his visitor. He put down the framed photo memory of happier times and pushed it back in its place. He did the same with the attacking feelings that he had let his family down.

"I promise I won't give up until I find you," he spoke to the picture. "I won't lose you as well," he determined.

Reinafox cleared his throat again. "Come in."

The door opened and two familiar faces popped their heads around it.

"Good morning," one of them smiled cheerfully. The

other one gave a quick wave.

"Kangarine, Crocarine." Reinafox nodded his greeting. Seeing these two always cheered him up.

"It's time for our special assembly and we need an inspiring word from our special leader," Kangarine smiled.

"Okay, how long have I got?"

"Five minutes." As Kangarine and Crocarine replied at the
same time, they gave each other that same knowing look.

"You twins crack me up!" Reinafox chuckled. "I'll be there in a minute."

"Sure," said Crocarine. "We'll go and start things off and we'll see you in there."

Reinafox straightened the papers that his speech was written on and tapped them on the stand in front of him as he came to the end of his talk. The room was silent as his audience listened carefully to his every word.

"As heroes, you must protect the innocent, help those in

need and be kind to those who have hurt you in the past, because hate only leads to more hate. We literally fought for the right to live in a world of love and justice." Reinafox paused to give them time to think about what he had just said.

"Your powers are a gift. Make sure that you use them for good. Use them to serve your community. At the end of the day, we all have a choice. We fought a war for the right to choose. Make sure you choose good and goodness will be your consequence." Reinafox looked a few of his students in the eye. Most of them did not look away.

"Finally, I just want to let tell you that I...," he looked around at his hero family. "I mean, we are very proud of all of you for wanting to be the next generation of heroes and leaders. We will give you everything we have and teach you all that we know. We believe in all of you."

Reinafox looked at his audience and smiled. "Believe in yourselves."

The students applauded energetically with gratitude, as he excused himself and left the twins to conduct the rest of the assembly. As Reinafox reached his office door, Foxaroo rushed behind him.

"Reinafox!" She took a breath and slowed down as he stopped and invited her inside the office. She closed the door behind her. "I just wanted to update you on the search for your little brother."

Reinafox made his way to his desk chair and gave her his full attention. Foxaroo's eyebrows tangled in a sad frown. She looked down for a moment and then looked at him again.

"The door-to-door search reached the Big City borders last night, but they didn't find anything yet. The Internet adverts haven't given us any successful leads yet either."

Reinafox glanced at the photo on his desk again, his heart aching. "What about the other missing kids?"

Foxaroo shook her head sadly. "Nothing yet." Her face suddenly set with determination.

"But we won't give up Reinafox! The search started this morning just outside the borders of the City. We have many volunteers – adults and children. No one will give up until we know what's happened to these missing young ones. You'll see your little brother again. Just don't give up hope." She smiled at him.

He smiled back weakly. "Thank you."

"You're welcome." She nodded at him as she left the room.

As the door closed, Reinafox sank back in his chair.

"If only they'd managed to tell me where they hid him before," he thought. His mind backtracked to the same moment that he had visited thousands of times before since the war.

…

It had been the middle of the day and Reinafox was almost at Peak Cross, a place just outside the Big City. Across the valley, the enemy troops were gathering, ready to strike at any moment. If they conquered the Big City, they would be able to rule all fusion beings. Reinafox and his fellow warriors could not allow that to happen. They were fighting so that justice, kindness and the greater good would prevail.

The enemy had a leader whom they always spoke about: Dragabadge. They had all heard lots about him, but few had ever actually seen him. He worked behind the scenes but had a growing army working to make his goal a reality: to rule the world and for all fusion beings to serve him.

Dragabadge's army was led by a sly and cunning commander. He had bullied many poor fusion beings out of their homes and stolen their land to build Dragabadge's kingdom. Those who served Dragabadge faithfully were rewarded, but those who refused to serve him as their leader were treated horribly and beaten. Those who escaped with their lives ran to the Big City for protection and told their horror stories of what they had been through.

The leaders from the Big City were the protectors of freedom. Reinacat and Panthox were not only fantastic parents to Bobfox and Reinafox, but they were also great leaders of the free world. They had sent many warning messages to Dragabadge's army, but they'd not been heard.

Dragabadge wanted a world where he was lord over all and he was violently making it happen. The leaders of the Big City prepared for war...

Reinafox squinted as he'd seen his parents afar off heading towards the meeting point as planned. They were quickly coming his way when all of a sudden, they'd turned aside.

"What's happening?" He was puzzled and headed towards them.

"He's here Panthox!" Reinacat said delighted. "I see him over there."
"Let's get to him quickly and let him know where Bobfox is. We don't how much time we have left before the battle begins," Panthox said very seriously. His wife nodded and they walked faster. Just as they were about to break into a run, they heard the most petrifying sound.

"Help! Help! Is anybody there?" The desperate voice screamed for dear life. "Help! Help!"

The couple ran towards the sound.

"Hello? We're here. Where are you?" Panthox shouted out.

As they came around the corner, they saw two big hairy arms clinging to the ground over a cliff edge. The poor being was about to fall to his death! Reinacat gasped at the sight.

"Hold on, we're almost there." As they began to run

faster, the desperate being, who was afraid to fall, suddenly stopped crying as a thick, red and pointy tail flew up from behind him and stuck into the ground in front of him.

Smirking, he calmly pulled himself up and stood firmly on his two feet. He stood taller than Panthox and Reinacat, looked them both in the eye and with a smug grin, he nodded in greeting and said, "Dragear, nice to see you."

Before they could respond, another voice spoke from behind.

"How long I have waited for this!"

They turned to face the voice they recognised too well. Then, in the blink of an eye, two black gigantic wings unfolded from the fusion being's back. They flapped in front so quickly that you could barely see them move...

"Dragalion!" Reinafox heard his parents shouting their enemy's name. He ran around the corner to see his parents whipped up in the tornado created by Dragalion's wings.

"Mum! Dad!" he cried. He saw the wind take them to the edge of the cliff and he knew deep down that he was not going to be able to change what was about to happen. His heart hurt.

Dragalion turned and looked him straight in the eye. "Long live Lord Dragabadge!" He suddenly stopped the 'Wings of Doom', and Reinafox's helpless parents caught his eye for a millisecond that seemed to go by in slow motion. Then they simply fell down the steep cliff edge to their impending death.

Reinafox's world crumbled in that one moment. At the same time, he knew he needed to run. Fast. He had no idea how, but his legs carried him away to safety. He was grieving but now he was also mad! He would not let them win! The freedom leaders were gone. He would now have to lead the fight against evil. He would make sure that his parents' death meant something.

…

Reinafox looked out of his office window blinking away the tears.

"Where did they hide you little brother?" His shoulders shook as he wept quietly.

Chapter 8

"Are we nearly there yet?" Wolfarilla asked eagerly.

Bobfox looked to Dragalion, waiting for his answer. They had been travelling for a week now. Dragalion knew all the best places to stop and rest. Their supplies from the supermarket had lasted and they still had plenty left. It was getting easier to travel as their backpacks were getting lighter. It was reassuring to travel with the certainty of reaching the Big City. Dragalion knew the way and it was so nice for him to lead them.

"These kids are so annoying!" Dragalion thought, as he made his way through some large, thick bushes. "I wish they would shut up! The sound of their constant blabbering is aggravating my mane off!" He scowled and sighed heavily. Then he put on the sweetest voice he could and encouraged his two young followers.

"Not long to go now my little friends. There's about a day of travel left. You've done very well to make it this far, very well indeed."

He turned around and rolled his eyes as he kept going ahead. "We'll stop soon for a break."

Bobfox and Wolfarilla smiled at each other with excitement. They would soon be entering the Big City. They were so lucky to have Dragalion.

The two best friends babbled on, excited about being so close to the Big City and to finding out about their parents. The journey had been so long, but now their dream was almost a reality. They had been resting for about an hour now. It was refreshing to kick back and relax for a while.

This meadow was the perfect calm spot. Dragalion knew the way well. The summer sky had enough clouds for them to spot shapes and pictures. They wondered out loud if their parents were looking at the sky as well... wherever they were.

Dragalion was sat on a rock across the way; shoulders hunched over and deep in thought. It had been about an hour since he sent the signal. He didn't hear his two new friends asking him a question.

"Dragalion?"

"Huh?"

"What do you think?" Wolfarilla asked again.

47

"About what?" He snapped out of his daydream.

"That cloud over there!" Bobfox said eagerly. "I see a TV, but Wolfy over here says it looks more like a door. We need you to settle the argument. Who do you agree with?"

Dragalion screamed inside with vexation. They needed to get to their destination soon or he would finish them off with the 'Wings of Doom.' He took in a giant breath and pretended to sound interested. "I think it looks like a TV."

Bobfox giggled. "I told you so!"

Wolfarilla folded his arms and looked back at the clouds. "Whatever!"

The two young fusion beings were completely unaware of their guide's grumpy mood.

When the pinky nail of his right paw vibrated, Dragalion quivered with excitement. His eyes glittered with joy. "He's here!" he thought. He stood up.

"I need to go to the toilet boys and I'm going to need a little time, if you understand what I mean." He winked at them and waited for their response.

48

"We understand," Bobfox nodded. "We'll wait for you here."

Once out of their sight, Dragalion practically ran to the meeting point. When he saw his faithful employee, he was able to be his true self. As he walked strong and tall towards his subject, Dragear stood as tall and as still as possible, looking straight ahead.

"Everything is going as planned. We are ready for you to arrive."

"Purrr-fect." Dragalion thought about what was about to happen. "There can be no more setbacks or mistakes, or else I don't know what will happen to you..." he warned.

Dragear gulped. "Y-yes sir, Master Dragalion sir."

"Off you go. We won't be long. Be ready or there will be consequences. Warn the others."

Dragear nodded and hurried off on being dismissed. Dragalion waited a little while longer before returning to his young company. They picked up their things and carried on their journey with new energy.

As the bushes and trees became thicker, it was getting

darker and darker. For the first time, Bobfox and Wolfarilla started to doubt the direction they were travelling in. "Are you sure this is the right way?" they asked.

"We're almost there my friends."

"I don't remember the Big City being so full of green," Wolfarilla thought out loud.

"We will be there in a few minutes, don't worry." Dragalion spotted the tree with the hidden lever at the side and making sure that he was ten steps ahead of them, pulled it towards him.

Before the young fusions could think, there was a WHOOSH! and a CRRRASH!! All of a sudden, they were trapped in a metal cage that had fallen from the sky!

"Hey!" Bobfox yelled. "What's going on?"

"Dragalion!" Wolfarilla cried out. "Help us!"

"Oh no! Use your powers! Save yourselves," Dragalion gasped sarcastically, pretending to care. Bobfox screeched and clanged at the metal over and over until he couldn't anymore, but nothing. Nothing! Not even a scratch. They were both seriously puzzled. Bobfox thought he could cut through anything with his special powers, but they were tightly trapped.

Suddenly, their confusion was interrupted by an evil snicker that turned into a villainous cackle. Dragalion was bent over and holding his belly making a noise they had never heard from him before. It didn't fit the character of the nice being that had been guiding them all this time, but then he looked at them and they froze. His eyes were big and a deep blood red that glowed in the dark and left them cowering. Wolfarilla got his spikes armed and ready in defence, but Dragalion opened up his gigantic, black wings and got ready to retaliate. "Really? Don't you remember what happened when we first met?" They did not recognise this voice. It was pure evil.

Wolfarilla lowered his hands. The spikes went back in. "What's going on?" he begged.

Dragalion went back to the lever and pushed it upwards. The trees and bushes ahead of them lifted to reveal a dark cave. There were three of the most unfriendly looking fusion beings Bobfox and Wolfarilla had ever seen stood in the doorway. Dragear stood very tall and straight, baring his scary sharp teeth and looking like he could break anybody in half if only given the command. His

51

dark eyes glared straight ahead. Then there was Bullolf, whose red, evil eyes stared directly at Bobfox and Wolfarilla while he scraped his back hooves and breathed heavily, ready to attack.

Hovering a little way off the ground with his black wings spread menacingly wide was Dragabull. He glowered at the cage, puffing smoke out of his black nostrils. They greeted their leader with a bow and headed towards the cage like evil soldiers.

Dragalion smiled coldly at his young and gullible followers. "Welcome home. It's not the Big City, but it's where you're staying until you agree to join the real army. Your parents fought to get rid of us. They may have won the last war, but we will rise again. You will serve on our side or be slaves for the rest of your lives."

"We… we trusted you!" Bobfox felt his heart aching. "Do you know what happened to our parents?"

"Why should I care about your stupid parents!" snarled Dragalion. He delighted in the pain he saw in the frightened kids' eyes.

"You'll never get away with this!" Bobfox shouted with determination.

"Of course I will," came the reply. "Who's going to stop me? These cages are specially designed. Your powers are useless against them."

"We trusted you!" Wolfarilla's mind spun like a tornado trying to deal with the betrayal.

Dragalion instructed his soldiers. "Get them out of my sight!" The two biggest soldiers lifted the cage and headed towards the dark cave. As the cage passed the evil commander, Bobfox and Wolfarilla stared in disbelief.

Dragalion didn't look at them again. "Put them with the others."

Chapter 9

"Remember, young students," Reinafox spoke seriously as he walked in between the students' desks. "With power comes great responsibility. You are not better than those who haven't discovered their power yet. You have a duty to protect those who are weaker than you, not bully them because you are stronger than them."

He walked to the front of the classroom and made an effort to look into as many eyes as he could. The students did not look away from him. They were eager to learn from him. They wanted his approval.

Reinafox continued. "As members of the School for Heroes, you must be examples for your community. Isn't that right Crocarine?"

The students turned around to see Crocarine respond to the question. He was stood up straight and serious, claws behind his back. He was ready to answer any questions to assist Reinafox in teaching this very important lesson.

"Of course, sir. It's our duty," he said, appearing just as serious about the topic as his leader.

The students turned their attention to the front again, where their teacher was writing something on the whiteboard. Reinafox finished and stepped aside.

YOU HAVE THE POWER TO CONTROL YOURSELVES

"Never forget this, students," Reinafox said loudly. "At first, they can seem out of control or hard to handle, but remember that you can learn to control them. We will teach you. Do you understand class?"

"Yes sir!" The class responded with spirit.

"Good." Reinafox gave a satisfied nod. "Right. Close your eyes and focus your mind on the area of your body that is the centre of your power."

The classroom fell completely silent as the students followed his instructions. The focus was so intense it seemed like the students were not moving. Reinafox took in a breath ready to give his next instruction, but before he could say a word, the school tannoy system buzzed loudly.

"Reinafox please come to the office. I repeat, Reinafox, can you please report to your office for an urgent matter?

Thank you."

He recognised the female voice as belonging to Foxaroo. He knew that it must be very important because she would never interrupt his teaching if it wasn't.

Crocarine had made his way to the front of the classroom where Reinafox was standing, just as Kangarine entered the classroom. The students had now lost their concentration and were looking at their teachers to see what was going on.

"Crocarine, you're in charge. Please take over the lesson and send them out to break on time if I'm not back," Reinafox instructed. "Kangarine?"

"Yes sir?"

"Stay here and support him."

"Yes sir."

"Students, apologies for having to go, but these two are some of the best. Make sure that you pay attention and give them your best."

Reinafox speed walked down the hall to his office. His

mind was racing, thinking about all the problems that could be happening. As he entered his office, Foxaroo looked up at him from his computer at his desk.

"We have some news about your brother. You need to see this," she said seriously as she got up. She offered him the chair.

Reinafox's heart beat faster as he rushed to take the seat.

"Have you found Bobfox?" There was hope in his voice. As he sat down, he saw the paused video of CCTV footage.

"Not exactly," Foxaroo replied. "This is CCTV footage from 'The Big Happy Shopper' mini supermarket just outside the Big City. There was a break-in, and the owner recognised Bobfox in the footage from our Missing Persons ads."
Reinafox was confused. Foxaroo could sense it. "Just press play," she directed.

It felt incredible to see Bobfox again, even if it was only on camera. Before now, Reinafox had no real evidence that his little brother was still alive. He wasn't alone anymore. He still had family out there. He was disappointed that he was watching his brother break into the store, but...

"He's discovered his powers!" Reinafox was amazed that he had such control over his powers already.

"When did this happen?" he wondered aloud. Suddenly, the image he saw made him freeze with fear. As the dark wings unfolded on the screen, he recognised the 'Wings of Doom.' His blood ran cold as he identified the dark and fiendish character that followed Bobfox and his friend into the store.

"Dragalion!" he gasped. His mind went straight back to the moment he had seen his parents fall to their deaths.

His eyes grew wide as he couldn't stop his imagination taking him to Bobfox's death as well. Was he about to lose his little brother for good?

He breathed a sigh of relief when the situation calmed down as he continued to watch. He grew suspicious as Bobfox and his friend appeared very friendly with the evil Dragalion as they left. They seemed to be following him.

"It's a trap!" Reinafox panicked. "We need to find out where they've gone." He raised his voice and looked at Foxaroo. "Now!"

She mirrored his concern in her face and her tone of voice. "I have a search team ready to go to this location now. I knew you'd want to go straight away."

Reinafox looked at her full of gratitude, not knowing what to say, but he knew she understood.

"So, what are we waiting for?" He got up from the desk. "Let's go."

Chapter 10

"Psssst! Wolfy! Are you awake?"

"Yeah. Can't sleep."

"How long have we been here now? I'm losing track of the time."

"It's been two weeks now Bobfox. Fourteen meals, one a day. Fourteen invitations to join Dragalion's army. Fourteen times we've turned him down..."

"You know, I really miss the sunlight. We haven't seen daylight since the day we were captured," Bobfox sighed weakly. He was still getting used to the lack of energy and his body was getting thinner. But he would rather feel the weakness in his body than give in to Dragalion.

"That evil trickster!" he thought angrily. Somehow, he needed to get revenge.

"I can't believe we trusted him!" Bobfox banged his fist against the cage bars.

"Save your energy," Wolfarilla warned. "We need it for

planning. We will get out of here. We just need the right plan."

"You're never going to get out," came a negative and mean voice out of the darkness. "None of us are."

"Don't listen to him, Wolfarilla! I'm with you guys. I'm not giving up either!" said the voice of encouragement, Grog. "I saw the guilt and desperation in the eyes of the poor fusion being that tricked me into being caught," he sighed heavily. "I will never be in that position, whatever it takes."

Grog was a clumsy looking animal fusion. He had a really long and pale-yellow neck in comparison to his green, yellow body, but he had powerful jumping legs that were always crouched and ready to pounce into action. He hadn't jumped since they'd caged him. There was no room. He had only succeeded in bashing his head and hurting his strong and powerful neck. He was Dragalion's latest capture and he had already been there for two and half days. He had taken a liking to Bobfox and Wolfarilla. He was determined to be free again too.

...

Reinafox was grateful for his search team. They had come here every day for the past two weeks in search of Bobfox and the other missing fusions. They had found nothing – no clues, no young fusion beings wandering around. Nothing. It was as though they had never been there. If it wasn't for the CCTV footage at the supermarket, they wouldn't have even known if Bobfox was alive or dead. There had to be a clue around here or something!

Reinafox was determined not to give up just yet, but he needed to keep his team positive as well so that they wouldn't give up searching.

A member of the search team paused, rubbed his tired eyes, and sighed heavily. "We've been searching this area for two weeks straight. There's nothing here! Maybe we should accept that we won't find young Bobfox here. They must have moved on, and so should we."

Reinafox called everyone to stop what they were doing and gather round him.

"I know that we've been searching for the past two weeks and found nothing, but let's persevere and not give in." Reinafox looked seriously into the eyes of as many of the volunteers that he could.

"Imagine that each one of these missing young fusions are one of your family members, your own blood. Would you want others to persevere or to give up on you?"

The search party remained silent, but it was an unspoken "yes" in answer to their leader's question. Reinafox continued.

"I can't explain it properly, but I know there's something

here that will lead us to Bobfox and hopefully the others. I don't know exactly what it is but when we find it, I will know. Please, continue to believe in my leadership and work alongside me in this mission and I'm sure we will find something. Let's take a snack break to refresh our bodies and minds but stay vigilant, because you never know when you may find the clue that leads to the missing fusions. Agreed?" he asked the group.

"Agreed," they replied together. The search team scattered about nearby and sat down to eat from their snack packs.

Foxaroo found a spot under a nearby tree that looked comfortable enough. She signalled to Reinafox for him to join her and he walked over to her. The strained worry lines on his forehead made her heart ache for him. She pointed her paw at the spot opposite her that she had saved for him to sit down. He sat down heavily and sighed. Foxaroo broke the silence.

"Come on leader. You need to keep up your strength as well. Eat," she commanded. She took off her backpack and brushed aside some twigs to clear a space to sit down.

As she sat down to eat, she felt and heard the crunch of something unusual underneath her. Face slightly

65

scrunched and nose twitching, she quickly got up again to investigate. There was some sort of wrapper. The way the light hit the silvery inside part of the wrapper made Foxaroo squint.

The way she picked up and inspected the wrapper intrigued Reinafox. She sniffed it and paused, then pondered and sniffed it again. There was something familiar about that smell!

"Hey, what have you got there?" Reinafox asked.
"It's like I know this smell, but I can't put my paw on it."

"Well, what does it smell like?" He moved to where she was.

Foxaroo sniffed at the wrapper again. "It kind of reminds me of you." She looked at Reinafox and handed him the wrapper, her face looking confused.

When he sniffed the wrapper, though the scent was faint, he recognised it immediately.

"Bobfox!" His eyes lit up with fresh hope and his body was suddenly full of new energy, as he sniffed intensely around the nearby trees and bushes to find out which direction Bobfox and his friends had gone in.

His search team looked on curiously, as their leader sniffed crazily around the area where he was. They knew that he had found a clue. Suddenly, everyone was re-energised even though they hadn't eaten much. They all rushed over to Reinafox and Foxaroo and started wildly asking questions.

"What have you found?" … "Is it Bobfox?" … "What can we do to help?"

Reinafox carried on his search for the scent and barely heard their questions. He was so focused on tracking it. It was faint, at least two weeks old but it was definitely Bobfox. He had to believe that he was near.

Foxaroo shushed the questioners. "Just give him a minute. He's picked up on Bobfox's scent. He needs to concentrate."

The team quietened down and looked on earnestly at Reinafox, hoping that he could figure out which direction to go in next. Suddenly, Reinafox stopped.

"I think he's found something!" Foxaroo said, full of hope.

The group almost held their breath while they waited for

Reinafox to speak.

"Found you!" he sounded thrilled, and his eyes lit up with excitement.

…

Dragear shoved the latest fusion being to give in to Dragalion's offer.

"Hurry up! We don't have all day."

Deereetah hated herself for giving into Dragalion, but she couldn't take the stench of that prison anymore and the hunger was killing her! She wished that there was another way of surviving. A hero to rescue her.

The guilt of tricking Grog into being captured was weighing her heart down like a rock. He had thought that she was his friend, but she'd betrayed him. She would never forget the look in his eyes as they took him away in the cage. Could she ever be forgiven? She didn't think there could be any forgiveness for what she had done.

Deereetah shook herself out of her deep thoughts. They were not getting her anywhere except deeper into her depression. If she didn't capture another clueless young fusion being today, she would find herself back in the cages. She hated the dark now. She just couldn't go back. She just couldn't.

All of a sudden, she realised that Dragear's breath was no longer on her back. He was always so close, there was no chance of escape. She looked over her shoulder to be met with those familiar dark and evil eyes. She jumped in fright.

"Don't even think about trying to run again. I'm always watching you," Dragear sneered barbarically in her ear. Her heart pounded as he reached out and touched the scar underneath her right eye.

"I can always do the other eye to match this one." He grinned, but it was sinister and cold. Deereetah said nothing. She didn't have to. They both knew that she was trapped. Just then, the silence was broken.

"Yoohoo! Dragear," cooed the familiar female voice that made him turn his head. "Hey sweetie."

"Rabbear!" he grinned. He loved her fluffy, long ears. Only she could be so bad and so cute at the same time.

"What are you doing here?" Deereetah noticed the change in his tone. She rolled her eyes behind his back but didn't move.

"I heard you were on guard duty out here, so I brought my lunch with a little extra. Do you want some?" Rabbear held up a small picnic basket and smiled that smile that made him want to do anything she said. He was torn, but he couldn't leave his prisoner. The punishment wasn't worth it.

"I can't stop for lunch right now," he called back. "But maybe I could have a little something from your basket as you've made the effort. Give me a second."

Dragear turned back to Deereetah and growled. "If you move from this very spot, you'll be dead meat," he sneered. "I'm watching you."

Deereetah watched as he met Rabbear a short distance away. She had no chance of escape. Rabbear touched Dragear's muscly arm, and he turned around so that he could keep an eye on Deereetah from where he was. There was rustling in the bushes next to her and before she could move, she heard a friendly voice.

"Don't freak out. Act normally. We're here to help."

Deereetah started to turn in the direction of the voice.

"Don't do anything to make him suspicious! Stay facing in his direction." The voice sounded urgent. She obeyed.

"My name is Foxaroo and I am here with Reinafox, son of Panthox and Reinacat, the leaders of the heroes who won the Great War. My friends and I have been watching you for a little while. Are you a prisoner with the other missing young fusion beings? Blink three times if following you can lead us to the others."

Deereetah blinked three times. Could it be? Could she have a chance to redeem herself?

"Good. I need you to follow exactly what I say because today is the day you will be free."

The dying hope in her heart suddenly came to life as Foxaroo spoke to her. Things were about to change…

Chapter 11

She'd never been great at acting but she was giving this all she had.

Foxaroo's eyes grew wide with shock. Her jaw dropped as she gripped onto the metal cage bars.

"What's going on?"

An evil cackle came from behind her. Dragear looked her in the eyes as he walked over to Deereetah and ruffled the front of her hair.

"Nice job," he grinned, still looking at Foxaroo. Then he traced the scar under her eye with his paw. Deereetah was too afraid to move.

"Maybe you won't get a matching scar today after all."

"Deereetah?" Foxaroo looked at her for a response, but Deereetah did not have the courage to look in her eyes. She hung her head in shame and sadness. This was like tricking Grog all over again. Her heart was heavy.

Foxaroo raised her shoulders and dropped them heavily while clenching her fists. Her force field did not appear. She tried again with more oomph, but it was useless. She looked at her paws for the fault and she heard Dragear's cackle again.

"Your powers don't work in our cages. We're not stupid. We know that you would try to use them against us. Now you will use them to serve in the best army in history under our great leader, Dragalion."

"I will NEVER join your army!" Foxaroo scowled at her captor.

"That's what they all say at first. Next thing you know, they give in to sense like Deereetah here." Deereetah wished that she could disappear.

"You'll never get away with this!"

Dragear smirked. "They all say that as well."

Just then, Dragabull crept in from the shadows. He grabbed Deereetah by the arm and brought her close to the cage. He took one side of the cage while Dragabull took the other, and they both started to push it towards the hidden cave lair.

Foxaroo growled defensively as she was taken into captivity. Her captors laughed and Deereetah kept her gaze on the floor.

Once they were inside, Deereetah was ordered to her living quarters and Foxaroo was taken in her cage to the underground prison where the others were held. She tried to pay close attention to where she was being taken. She was also scanning for weaknesses, which became hard once it got dark. She noted the short ride down in the lift and a few right-hand turns and then... the smell!

"Urrrgh!" Foxaroo retched. She covered her mouth with her paw. It was all she could do not to vomit. She'd never smelt anything like it! She had to get out of there.

She was wheeled into a room where the smell was the strongest. Her cage was slotted in place next to another with a bang and a clang. She heard the heavy footsteps walking away, the slam of a heavy door being shut and the sound of an automatic locking system. Then silence.

"Hello?" she said into the dark. "Is anybody here?" She listened carefully.

"We're all here," the negative voice spoke back sarcastically.

"Bobfox? Is Bobfox here?" Foxaroo enquired.

Bobfox was sat still. He was conserving his energy, working on his escape plan in his head as he did daily. His ears sprang upright when he heard his name. "Someone knows I'm here?" he thought.

"Who are you?" he asked out loud.

Foxaroo wanted to make sure that it was really him and not a trick. She had to get it right.

"I'm someone that Bobfox will really want to know right now. If you are him, I can tell you more, but I need to make sure. Are you Bobfox?"

Bobfox decided he had nothing to lose. "Yes, I am, but how are you going to prove that?"

"Tell me about your siblings," she said.

Thinking about his brother made him sad. This search seemed to be taking forever. He sighed.

"I have one brother... well, I had one brother. I had parents too. They hid me away when they went to fight in the Great War but none of them came back for me. I was heading to the Big City to find out what happened to them, even if it was bad news..." He paused briefly. Then he got angry.

"Then we were tricked into being captured and now I'm working on a plan to get out of here!" He made a fist and punched the cage bars. He calmed down his breathing again and turned to the direction of the new voice. "Now, enough about me. Tell me who you are."

The more Bobfox spoke, the more excited Foxaroo became. He was so much like his brother – hoping against hope and so determined! Those were some of the characteristics that she loved about Reinafox. She had seen his sadness of losing his parents and not being able to find his brother, and now she was going to lead the rescue mission that would reunite them!

"What is your brother's name?" she asked, already knowing the answer.

Bobfox smiled at the memories that his brother's name brought to mind. "Reinafox," he sighed. "His name is Reinafox."

Chapter 12

Each of the prisoners listened carefully to their new leader, as she explained the plan over the next hour or so. They gave her the information she needed and rehearsed their parts to play back to her over and over again. Though she was in the dark and knew that her comrades couldn't see her, she stood up and gestured passionately as though they could. This whole nightmare was about to be over.

"Right! I think we're all set!" she said. "Let's preserve our energy and wait for my signal. I believe in each and every one of you and I am proud of you Grog. You've all come out of your negativity. We will all be free with your help," Foxaroo said firmly. "You're heroes."

No one could see in the darkness, but Grog smiled for the first time since he had been captured.

After some time, they heard the familiar footsteps of the daily visit of the offer to join the dark side.

"Places everyone!" Foxaroo hissed.

The doors buzzed and clicked as they opened. The lights came on and Dragalion entered, walking tall on his hind legs. His chest was all puffed up and his head held high like royalty. His ugly henchmen, Dragabull and Dragear, followed sinisterly. He stopped halfway down the corridor and started his usual speech and offer.

Grog looked him up and down while his belly rumbled and waited for him to finish. He was so hungry and so ready for this.

"Join me and tonight, you will eat like kings," Dragalion boasted, looking around. He looked at Foxaroo. "Or Queens," he added.

"Urgh!" she snorted in reply.

Dragalion carried on, ignoring her. "Your time is running out. We'll soon have the greatest army in history. Don't you want to be on the winning side?"

The silence irritated him. He nodded at his henchmen as he began to walk out. "Your loss. Let's go."

"I'll join you."

Dragalion heard the quiet voice and turned around. "Who said that?"

"It's me, Grog," he said a bit louder.

Dragalion grinned. "They all give in eventually."

He pointed to Grog's cage and ordered Dragear. "Get him out. Take him upstairs and get him cleaned up."

"Traitor!" Bobfox shouted at Grog. He hoped he sounded convincing. "I thought we were friends!"
Grog said nothing as Dragear went to wave his card over the electric lock and opened it up. He led him out by the elbow. Grog moved slowly and weakly out of the cage.

"You definitely made the right choice," Dragalion sneered. "A soldier needs to be strong," he deliberately said loud enough for the others to hear.

Grog nodded slowly. "I wasn't before, but I'm ready now."

Dragalion smiled that evil smile.

Bobfox shouted angrily. "Oh! You're ready now, are you?"

"That's what I said!" Grog said louder. He looked at Foxaroo and continued. "I'm ready NOW!"

At the same time as Grog's "NOW," Foxaroo held down

the precious stone on the silver ring hidden under the fur of her right paw.

In an instant, the room went dark and the buzz of electricity suddenly stopped as all the cage doors flew open at once. Grog saw the shock and panic on Dragear's face through the shadows, as he wrapped his powerfully

long tongue around his arms and waist, lifting him past his powerful neck and above his head.

Before he had a chance to shout for help, Grog jumped for the first time since being captured. It felt so good to jump again, but Dragear wasn't feeling anything now as he had been knocked unconscious from the impact of his head hitting the ceiling.

Grog carefully laid his body in one of the cages. He looked over the bully's body and smiled. "I was SO ready to do that!"

In that same moment, Dragabull began charging at Grog with full force. Wolfarilla stretched out his fists for the first time since he first saw Dragalion and thought he and Bobfox were in danger. He felt pumped up as the pointy spikes stood on end. His heart pounded like a drum. He was so excited to be free; they were all going to be free! He was going to play his part well. He pointed his fists in the direction of his target.

The raging bull barely had time to take a breath before he was stopped in his tracks and carried through the air in the opposite direction by a thousand spikes stuck into the edges of his clothes. He hit the wall with a thud, as he was pinned to it by Wolfarilla's spikes. His mouth fell open in shock and surprise. The more Dragabull struggled, the more it seemed that he was stuck to the wall. He grunted wildly and huffed and puffed, but it was no use.

Wolfarilla punched the air with excitement. "Yessssssss!" he shouted triumphantly.

Bobfox was grateful for his night vision, as he saw very well even in the dark. It wasn't totally clear in that dungeon, but it was clear enough for him to see that Dragalion was no longer in the room. He growled.

"He's gone!" he exclaimed to Foxaroo. "We can't let him get away!"

"Is everyone okay?" Foxaroo checked in with her new crew. They replied with a mixture of nods and yeses.

"C'mon," she led the way. "Let's get out of here."

As they burst through the doors upstairs, Foxaroo looked for her new friend.

"Deereetah!" she shouted. "Are you okay?" She couldn't see her for a minute, but then she heard the sound of running and shuffling feet.

"Foxaroo?" It was Deereetah.

"We're over here. Is everyone okay?"

Deereetah made her way to where Foxaroo was standing. "We're all fine. The guards are tied up back there. Can we get out of here now please?"

"You guys are really alright? Didn't Dragalion come your way?" she questioned. The worry was in her voice and her face. She remembered what he had done with his big, black wings when she had seen the CCTV footage.

Deereetah was alarmed at the thought that Dragalion could be lurking around waiting for the right moment to pounce on them. Her eyes squinted as she scanned the room, looking for signs of danger.

"I didn't see him," she said still looking around. "He didn't come our way."

"Let's head out." Foxaroo pointed towards the direction of the exit. At that same moment, she heard a familiar voice calling her name and she saw flickers of light as though from many torches. Relief ran through her body. They were all going home!

Bobfox heard the voice calling for Foxaroo. He didn't really recognise it, but it sounded familiar.

"Are you all safe?"

"Yes, our plan was almost perfect," Foxaroo replied. "We're making our way out."

"Have you got my brother?" Reinafox held his breath.

Bobfox's ears pricked up and twitched.

"Reinafox?" he said to himself out loud.

Reinafox heard and called out before he could stop himself. "Bobfox!"

"Reinafox!" Bobfox cried out.

Foxaroo interrupted. "I guess you know now." She smiled as she called across the room. "But we don't know where Dragalion is! He may have escaped."

Reinafox's paws made fists and he clenched his teeth at the mention of Dragalion's name. He felt as though he would explode with anger. First his parents and now his brother. He had to bring him to justice! He wanted to hug his little brother so tightly and never let go again, but if he saw him right now, he would lose the chance to catch that dirty murderer, Dragalion. He couldn't let that happen.

"Foxaroo, get everybody out to safety," he instructed. "The team and I will take it from here."

"Alright," she called back. "Be careful and I'll see you outside." She started to make her way to the entrance.

"Come on guys. Stay together and be on the lookout. We're almost there." Reinafox instructed his rescue crew.

"Don't worry," said Foxaroo. "He'll be fine. He's a good fighter and he's not alone. His team is the best. You will see him again."

Bobfox didn't want to move, but Foxaroo grabbed his arm.

"Come on. We have to go before anyone gets hurt. Some of us are still really weak."

Reinafox and his team scoured the whole cave complex from top to bottom. The guards were handcuffed with power-neutralising cuffs and lined up at mouth of the cave, waiting to be taken to the Big City prison. Foxaroo looked with satisfaction.

"Now you'll have plenty of time to consider what you've done to these innocent fusion beings while you're in prison."

Chapter 13

Reinafox was the last to come out to the front of the cave. He let out the biggest sigh as he walked over to Foxaroo. He shook his head.

"He's gone! We've looked all over the place and he's not here." Hot tears ran from his eyes. Foxaroo rubbed his back gently with her paw.

"He's escaped." He wanted to get justice to honour his parents, but that wasn't going to happen now.

Foxaroo looked him in the eye. "You've done all you could have done up to now and look at the results of that." She pointed in the direction of the escaped young fusions.

"If it wasn't for you not willing to give up the search, they would have been in captivity until now."

Reinafox looked around and took in the victory. Who knows what would have happened if he and his team hadn't come here today? His gaze stopped at the sight he had been waiting to see for so long. His heart beat fast with love and joy, so much joy. Now the tears flowed again but with happiness this time.

"I think there is someone else that needs your focus and attention right now, don't you?" Foxaroo gave him a gentle push towards his no longer lost little brother.

Meanwhile a dark, shadowy figure looked on from nearby high ground. He paced up and down, silently boiling with indignation. The earpiece he wore vibrated with the sound rushing from it.

"You idiotic, useless fool!" it boomed. "We were so close and you blew it! I can't come back now. You've lost my army!"

Dragalion did his best to sound humble. "Yes, your highness. You are right. I apologise for my failure. I will accept any punishment you send my way. Please, give me another chance and I won't fail."

Dragalion didn't like this feeling of fear at all. It was all Reinafox's fault. Again! He wanted revenge.

"Make your way back here and make sure that you are not followed. Am I clear?" the voice growled.

"Yes, Lord Dragabadge," he started. "I will not be followed."

"If I even think that you've been followed, you're on your own." Click. The line went dead.

"Curse you, Reinafox!" Dragalion spat as he ranted to himself, careful not to make too much noise for fear of being caught. That frustrated him even more. He was supposed towin this time! He breathed deeply as he glared at Reinafox and his team.

"You may have won this battle, but I'll be back and next time you won't be laughing. I got rid of your parents and I'll get rid of you too. Just you wait," he vented. He extended his wings and silently flew upwards until he was above the clouds and out of sight.

...

Bobfox sat on the ground with his head in his paws. The area was lit with what seemed like 100 torches. He remembered sitting in the hideout in the same position day after day, waiting for his parents or brother to come and rescue him. It felt as though that was years ago now. Here he was again, waiting for his brother to come. Before he could think another thought, he smelled a familiar scent and was covered by a tall shadow.

Reinafox couldn't stop the tears from flowing, as he walked up to the sight he had been longing to see for so long. The only family he had left had been gone without a trace for so long, but now they were finally about to be reunited.

Reinafox stretched out a paw to his little brother's shoulder. Bobfox stood up and turned around in that same moment. There was so much he wanted to say to his big brother but when he looked into his eyes, he felt so many emotions bubbling inside. All he managed to say was, "I've been looking for you for so long." Then all his feelings came out at once.

Before he broke down in a flood of tears, Reinafox embraced him and held him up as his shoulders shook while he cried. Reinafox cried too, but he wanted to make his brother feel safe at the same time.

After a long hug, Reinafox broke hold to look Bobfox in his face. "We've got a lot to catch up on." He smiled.

Bobfox wiped his eyes and smiled back blissfully. "I've got so much to tell you."

The energy was coming back to his voice. "I've got so much to ask you." He paused for a moment. "Where's Mum and Dad?" he inquired.

The sadness that took over his big brother's face confirmed his fear. Reinafox put an arm around Bobfox's shoulders and began to tell the story of one of the worst days of his life.

Foxaroo looked on at the family reunion with a tear in her eye. It made her so happy to see that his pain was now over. Reinafox was such a good fusion being. And handsome too, but she would never say that out loud. She remembered seeing him go through all the pain of searching for Bobfox. She felt so sad for him. But through his pain, he continued to lead the recovery from the war and to build the School for Young Heroes. He was her hero and Bobfox was a lot like him. Now they were together, a family team. Their bond was already strong, but no one could break it now. They would be inseparable.

Wolfarilla looked at his new best friend with his brother. They were a family again. He was delighted for them both, but he still felt a little sad that he hadn't found his own family yet. He wanted so much to feel what Bobfox was feeling now, but he couldn't. He had started daydreaming about being a part of a family again when he was interrupted.

"Reinafox, meet my best friend, Wolfy." Bobfox grinned at his adventure buddy. "I wouldn't have gotten through everything without him."

Reinafox stuck out his paw to shake Wolfarilla's hand. Wolfarilla responded.

"Well, I guess that makes him part of the family." Reinafox smiled warmly, looking into his eyes. Suddenly, Wolfarilla didn't feel so lost anymore.

"If it's okay with you, we would love you to stay with us and help you to find your family."

Wolfarilla fought the tears that were trying to fall. "I would like that very much. Thank you."

So, the two best friends and their shared big brother were joined by Foxaroo, sitting on the grassy ground waiting for the rescue vehicles to take them home. Bobfox could barely believe all that he had gone through on this crazy adventure, and he was so glad that it was over. But he would gladly do it all over again because he had found his family. Whatever happened next, he could face it. He wasn't alone.

Glossary of Animal Fusions (in order of appearance)

Bobfox: bobcat/fox

Reinafox: reindeer/fox

Wolferine: wolf/wolverine

Coyolf: coyote/wolf

Orangacoon (the angry farmer): orangutan/raccoon

Wolfarilla: wolf/gorilla

Dragalion: dragon/lion

Kangarine: kangaroo/wolverine

Crocarine: crocodile/wolverine

Foxaroo: fox/kangaroo

Dragabadge: dragon/badger

Reinacat: reindeer/cat

Panthox: panther/fox

Dragear: dragon/bear

Bullolf: bull/wolf

Dragabull: dragon/bull

Grog: giraffe/frog (a character created by Sawyer Brooks)

Deereetah: deer/cheetah

Rabbear: rabbit/bear

Printed in Great Britain
by Amazon

14675285R00061